THIS BOOK BELONGS TO:

Yogi Bear and related characters are trademarks of
Hanna-Barbera Productions, Inc.

Published by Bedrock Press™, an imprint of Turner Publishing, Inc.,
A Subsidiary of Turner Broadcasting System, Inc.,
1050 Techwood Drive N.W., Atlanta, Georgia 30318.

Distributed by Andrews and McMeel,
A Universal Press Syndicate Company,
4900 Main Street, Kansas City, Missouri 64112.

Distributed in Australia by Pan Macmillan Australia Pty Limited,
Level 18, St. Martins Tower, 31 Market Street, Sydney.

Distributed in the U.K. by Pegasus Sales and Distribution Limited,
Unit 5B, Causeway Park, Wilderspool Causeway,
Warrington, Cheshire WA4 6QE.

Manufactured in the United States of America
10 9 8 7 6 5 4 3 2 1

LOST AND FOUND

Written by Ronald Kidd
Illustrated by John Kurtz

Bedrock Press

On a very rainy day in Jellystone Park, most of the animals were very happy. Rabbits hopped through the meadow, playing tag with the raindrops. Birds splashed in the puddles and sang in the showers. Spiders spun webs that sparkled in the mist like tiny strings of pearls.

Yogi Bear stood at the entrance to his cave with his little friend Boo Boo, gazing out at the gray skies.

"I'm tellin' you, Boo Boo, on a day like today, your ol' pal Yogi is sadder than the average bear."

"But why, Yogi?" asked Boo Boo.

"You see, it's like this," Yogi replied. "When it rains, it pours. When it pours, the tourists stay inside. And when the tourists stay inside, so do their pic-a-nic baskets. In other words, Boo Boo, every time it gets wet, my food supply dries up!"

The two friends tried playing cards to pass the time. But when Yogi looked at his cards, all he could see was the jack of club sandwiches and the ace of steaks.

"It's no use," he said finally. "I just can't think, 'cause my tummy's on the blink!"

"But Yogi, you should be happy," Boo Boo replied.

"I should?"

"Sure!" said Boo Boo. "Didn't you notice? The sun just came out!"

High above Jellystone Park, a rainbow blazed across the sky. It started at the distant treetops and ended at a familiar spot just below Yogi's cave — the picnic area! Already, carloads of tourists were lined up to get in.

"Is it true what they say?" asked Boo Boo. "Is there really a pot of gold at the end of the rainbow?"

Yogi grinned. "Right now I'd settle for a *pot roast*. Stick with me, Boo Boo, we've got work to do!"

As they approached the picnic area, a horn honked, and Ranger Smith pulled up in his jeep.

"Now, fellows, you know the rules," he said.

"Rules?" said Yogi. "What rules?"

Ranger Smith pointed to a sign that said DO NOT FEED THE BEARS. "Just a little reminder. I don't want any picnic baskets disappearing."

Yogi grinned. "There's no need to fuss. You can count on us!"

Yogi and Boo Boo strolled into the picnic area and saw a young couple with two dogs, preparing for a picnic. Yogi spotted a basket left all alone on the table.

"Remember what Ranger Smith said," Boo Boo warned. "It's against the rules to take picnic baskets."

"Boo Boo, ol' buddy, how do we know it's a pic-a-nic basket? Maybe it's a shopping basket. Maybe it's a sewing basket. You just never know."

"Yogi—" But it was too late. Before Boo Boo could say another word, Yogi had tiptoed to the table, grabbed the basket, and dashed into the woods.

Back at the cave, Yogi brought out his best tablecloth, and he and Boo Boo sat down to lunch with the basket between them. "Get ready to eat, 'cause you're in for a treat!" Yogi said gleefully.

"So, what do you think, Boo Boo? Do we have fried chicken? Potato salad? Maybe some nice chocolate cake?" asked Yogi. When he lifted the cover, Yogi found out that they didn't have any of those things. Instead, they had a puppy.

Sadly, Yogi shook his head. "Boo Boo, this place is going to the dogs."

"Look at the bright side, Yogi," grinned Boo Boo. "It wasn't a picnic basket, so we didn't break any rules."

The puppy wagged his tail and hopped out of the basket.

"I'll bet his family misses him," said Boo Boo. "We'd better take him back."

Yogi brightened. "Right you are, Boo Boo. After all, how else can we get another pic-a-nic basket?"

They returned just in time to see the young couple driving away. Yogi ran as fast as he could, but when they saw a bear chasing their car, they sped up and disappeared around the bend.

"I guess we could leave the puppy here," said Boo Boo, "but what if they don't come back?"

"Boo Boo," sighed Yogi, "I hate to say it, but I think we've just found a new roommate!"

Before they went home, Yogi swiped a picnic basket from another table. This time, he checked inside first. His eyes lit up, and he sang out, "I think I spy a pizza pie!"

At last, Yogi and Boo Boo got their lunch, and so did the puppy. Watching the little dog eat, Yogi chuckled, "He likes pepperoni. I guess that makes him a pupperoni!"

And that's what they called him — Pupperoni.

Later that afternoon, Cindy Bear stopped by for a visit. "You are the cutest thing I've ever seen!" she said.

Yogi grinned. "You know what they say, Cindy. I'm cuter than the average bear!" It wasn't long before Yogi figured out that Cindy Bear was talking about Pupperoni.

Cindy hugged Pupperoni and scratched him behind the ears. She was having so much fun that she barely even glanced at Yogi. Watching her, Yogi got an idea, and the idea became a master plan.

"Yogi Bear," he said to himself, "you are a pic-a-nic genius!"

The next day, Yogi took Pupperoni to the picnic area and set him loose on the grass. The tourists, eating at tables nearby, did exactly what Cindy had done — they all went over to play with Pupperoni. They were having such a good time that they didn't notice the bear with the funny hat strolling among the tables and collecting their picnic baskets.

In the park office, Ranger Smith's phones were ringing off the hook. Tourists were calling from all over the park, complaining about a puppy. It seemed that wherever the puppy appeared, picnic baskets disappeared.

"Sandwiches missing?" said Ranger Smith into one phone.

"Potato chips?" he said into another. "Brownies? Cookies? Candy bars? Yes, ma'am, I'll check into it right away. And I think I know exactly where to look!"

RANGER SMITH
RANGER

Ranger Smith hopped into his jeep and sped off through the forest. Within minutes, he pulled up to Yogi Bear's cave, where dozens of baskets were stacked.

Trying to control his temper, he said, "Yogi, I'd like you to explain what these are. And it had better be good."

"Why, sir, they're pic-a-nic baskets," Yogi replied. "Don't they teach you that in ranger school?"

"By the way," Yogi said, "what kind of meat do you like?"

"Well, I'm fond of ham," said Ranger Smith.

"On white, whole wheat, or rye?"

Ranger Smith exploded. "I don't want a sandwich! Those sandwiches belong to our visitors, and I'm taking them back!"

The ranger loaded up his jeep with the baskets. "No more picnic baskets, do you hear? Oh, and if you see a puppy around here anyplace, bring him in."

As Ranger Smith drove off, Yogi called after him, "No more pic-a-nic baskets — yes, sir, you got it!" Waving to the ranger, Yogi chuckled to himself, "I'm lettin' it slide, 'cause I've got more inside!"

But when Yogi walked back into the cave, he was shocked. Empty picnic baskets littered the floor. Lying in the middle of them was Pupperoni, patting his very, very full tummy.

Meanwhile, miles away, Mark and Sally Johnson were just getting home from their vacation in Jellystone Park. They unpacked the car, then opened up the trailer where they kept their three dogs. Mitzi came out. Spike came out. But where was little Scooter?

"Check Scooter's basket," Sally said. "I'll bet he's asleep."

They both searched the trailer, desperate to find Scooter. "The basket's not here," said Mark. "Come to think of it, I haven't seen it since our last picnic."

"We must have left Scooter behind!" wailed Sally. "What are we going to do?"

There was only one thing *to* do. They loaded their two dogs into the trailer and drove back to Jellystone Park.

In Jellystone Park, Yogi, Boo Boo, and Pupperoni set out for Cindy Bear's cave. They found her working in the garden.

"Hey-hey-hey, it's a beautiful day!" called Yogi.

Boo Boo chimed in, "We're taking a walk to Inspiration Point. Would you like to join us?"

Pupperoni licked Cindy's hand, and she smiled. "I'd love to, as long as Pupperoni comes along!"

PICNIC AREA

They set off through the woods. After a while Cindy asked, "Yogi, why are we taking the long way to Inspiration Point?"

Yogi replied, "To get some inspirational pic-a-nic baskets!"

Sure enough, up ahead was a picnic area. As they drew near, Pupperoni's ears perked up, and he took off running.

"Hey, Pupperoni, wait!" called Yogi. "You're barkin' up the wrong tree!"

They followed the little dog to the picnic area, where he ran past Ranger Smith and straight into the arms of Mark and Sally Johnson.

"No, Yogi," said Boo Boo. "I think it's the right tree."

Pupperoni jumped on Mitzi and Spike, and the three dogs rolled happily in the grass.

"I wonder what he's been doing all this time," Sally said.

"We've had lots of puppy sightings over the last day or so," said Ranger Smith. "I'd say he's been pretty busy."

Mark rubbed the little dog's tummy, which was fat and round. "I thought he'd be hungry," said Mark, "but it looks like he's gained weight!"

Just then, Sally glanced up and noticed Yogi peeking out from behind a tree. "That bear!" she exclaimed.

Ranger Smith chuckled. "Don't worry about Yogi, ma'am. He won't hurt you."

"Oh, I wasn't really afraid," she said. "It's just that I recognize him. He's the bear who chased our car as we were leaving."

"He must have been trying to tell us we forgot our puppy," said Mark.

Yogi stepped out from behind the tree, followed by Cindy and Boo Boo. He was greeted by Mitzi, Spike, and Pupperoni.

"We tried to take care of your puppy while you were gone," said Yogi. "I hope you don't mind."

"Mind!" said Sally. "How can we ever thank you?"

Yogi thought for a moment and said, "Well, to start with, could you do something about those signs?"

DO NOT FEED THE BEARS

The Johnsons packed up their trailer again and drove off down the road, this time making sure Pupperoni was with them.

"You know, there's just one thing that puzzles me," said Ranger Smith. "Since bears aren't supposed to be in the picnic area, how did you come across that puppy in the first place?"

"Oh, it's a long story, sir," Yogi replied.

"Let's just say . . . I'm smarter than the average bear!"

Late that afternoon, Yogi, Cindy, and Boo Boo watched the sunset from Inspiration Point.

"You know," Yogi said, "I'm gonna miss that little guy."

"Me, too," sighed Boo Boo.

Cindy said, "All of us will. But at least we know he's back where he belongs, with his family and friends."

"Boo Boo, ol' buddy," said Yogi, "you remember that rainbow we saw? It really did have a treasure at the end."

"It did?" asked Boo Boo.

"Yessiree, but it wasn't a pot of gold. It wasn't even a pot roast. It was Jellystone Park. That's the best treasure of all, because it's where *my* friends live."

Cindy put her head on Yogi's shoulder, and Boo Boo snuggled up close. Together, they watched the beautiful glow from the sunset spread slowly across their home.